This is dedicated to
two silly geese named Jane and Billy
and to the doctors and nurses at Children's Hospital. All the
money I earn from the sale of this book (and I bet it'll be a LOT!)
will be donated to CHLA and children's hospitals around the country.

—J.K.

All rights reserved. Published in the United States by Random House Children's Books,
a division of Penguin Random House LLC, New York.

Random House and the colophon are registered trademarks of Penguin Random House LLC.

Visit us on the Web! rhcbooks.com

Educators and librarians, for a variety of teaching tools, visit us at RHTeachersLibrarians.com

Library of Congress Cataloging-in-Publication Data is available upon request.
ISBN 978-0-525-70775-2 (trade) | ISBN 978-0-525-70777-6 (lib. bdg.) |
ISBN 978-0-525-70776-9 (ebook)

MANUFACTURED IN CHINA
10 9 8 7 6 5 4 3 2 1
First Edition

The SERIOUS GOOSE

WRITTEN AND ILLUSTRATED BY
JIMMY KIMMEL

Random House 🏠 New York

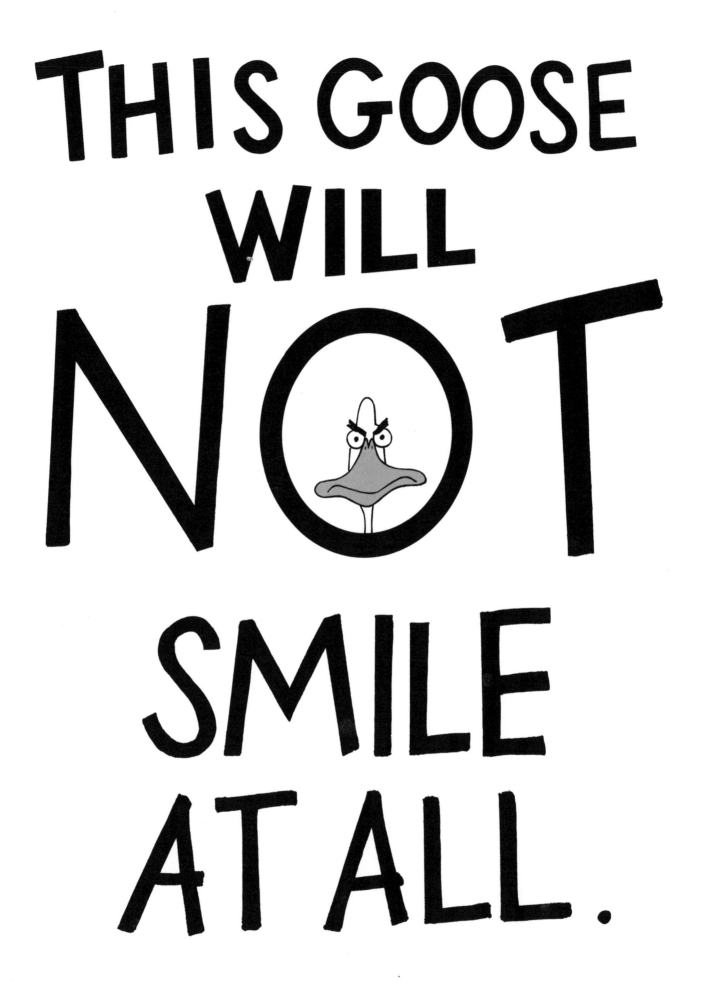

NOT EVEN IF YOU PUT A CHICKEN...

Even if you
ORDER A

PIZZA...

This goose means
BUSINESS.

SERIOUS business.
NO ONE
CAN MAKE THIS GOOSE SMILE!

What's that you say?

You think **YOU**

can do it ?

But go right ahead.
LOOK in the MIRROR
and GIVE IT A SHOT

MAKE FUNNY FACES
LET'S SEE WHAT YOU'VE GOT

STICK OUT YOUR TONGUE
AND LET YOUR EARS WIGGLE

ACT LIKE A MONKEY
THIS GOOSE SHALL NOT GIGGLE

CLUCK LIKE A CHICKEN
MOO LIKE A COW

BE DOOFY, BE GOOFY
ANY WAY YOU KNOW HOW

HOWEVER YOU DO IT,
IT WON'T BE ENOUGH

THIS GOOSE ISN'T SILLY
THIS GOOSE IS TOO TOUGH!

SEE?

I HATE TO SAY I TOLD YOU SO,
BUT THIS IS EXACTLY WHAT
I KNEW WOULD HAPPEN.

GOOD TRY, THOUGH.
YOU WERE VERY FUNNY.

MOST GEESE
WOULD HAVE LAUGHED SO HARD,
EGGS WOULD BE COMING OUT.

BUT NOT THIS GOOSE.

THIS GOOSE WILL NEVER, EVER...

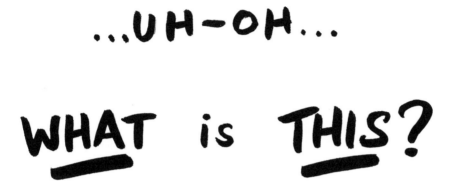

THIS IS
TERRIBLE.

BY THE
POWER
VESTED IN ME

BY THE ORDER OF
SERIOUS
GEESE AND GOOSES,

I HEREBY
COMMAND
YOU TO...

WOW!

THE GOOSE IS **REALLY** GIGGLING!

THIS IS **NOT** SUCH A SERIOUS GOOSE AFTER ALL.

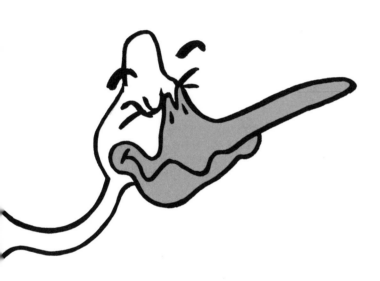

IN FACT, THIS **SEEMS TO BE...**

YOU

ARE A SILLY KID.

You'll be hearing from our attorneys.